THE WIZARD COMES TO TOWN
Written and illustrated by MERCER MAYER

For Ram Dass, a very fine wizard indeed

A RAINBIRD BOOK

First **RAINBIRD** Edition 1991
Printed in Italy

One day a stranger appeared at Mrs. Beggs's boarding house looking for a room to rent. His calling card read

Z.P. ALABASIUM
Wizard Extraordinaire

"This room suits me fine," he said. "I'll take it." He gave Mrs. Beggs a month's deposit and she gave him the key.

That evening Mr. Alabasium didn't show up for dinner
so Mrs. Beggs fixed him a tray of food and took it
up to his room.

"Just leave it on the floor, Mrs. Beggs," he said,
not bothering to open the door.
"Dear me," she said and went down the stairs.

That night as she lay in bed, she heard strange noises
from the room above. Up the stairs crept Mrs. Beggs,
followed closely by all the guests who had also
heard the noises.

"Oh my, what can be happening?" she said, knocking
on Mr. Alabasium's door.

"Nothing to concern yourself with, Mrs. Beggs,"
said Mr. Alabasium. "Now leave me be." With that
he slammed the door shut.

That would have suited Mrs. Beggs just fine, for
she wasn't a particularly nosey person.
However, the next morning she found the fresh
cut flowers on the dining room table withered and
dead. Oh well, I'll cut some more, she thought,
and went outside.
In the backyard, her beautiful garden was overgrown
with weeds, thistles and briars. To make matters
worse, the birdbath was full of toads.

As if that wasn't enough, a giant windstorm
came up that afternoon just as Mrs. Beggs was
hanging out the laundry. With a swoosh and a swirl,

Mrs. Beggs and the fresh clean laundry were blown
all over the yard.
But even stranger things were yet to happen.

The following day a rainstorm thundered through
the parlor, soaking everyone to the bone.

"Oh, I'm so sorry," cried Mrs. Beggs. "It has never rained in here before."

At lunch the tables and chairs floated through
the air. The dishes and fine china fell off
the shelves.

Old man Blagget's wheelchair flew out the
front door carrying poor old man Blagget far
across town.

Grannie Appleton's cane turned into a snake and slithered away. Of course, Grannie Appleton screamed.

Strange things wandered through the house or
just floated through the air frightening the guests.

Mr. Plimp's beaver hat turned back into a beaver
and bit Mr. Plimp on the nose.

Mrs. Fizzle found reptiles in her bed and fainted.
Needless to say, the guests were very unhappy
and complained.

To make matters even worse, a blizzard raged
into the house, howling and blowing snow
everywhere. "Mrs. Beggs," said Major Clearlob,

"I believe I can speak for the rest of the guests.
That Mr. Alabasium is up to no good. Either
he goes or we go."

Oh, dear, thought Mrs. Beggs. This is
becoming very bad for business. I must find out
if Mr. Alabasium is up to no good or not.
"Mr. Alabasium," she said knocking on his door,
"I was wondering if..." But before she finished
talking she found herself dressed in a ballet
costume, standing on a giant turtle.
"Oh, dear," she said. "This must stop."
So she called the constable.

The constable came and knocked on the door.
"Open up, this is the constable."

Suddenly the constable turned into a ram.
"Baaaaaaaaa," he said and ran down the stairs.

"That does it," Mrs. Beggs said angrily. She went
to her closet. She opened the door.
Reaching high up in the closet she pulled down
an old tattered box from the top shelf.
This may not be the right thing to do, she thought,
but one must do something. The top of the box read

WITCHERY FOR FUN AND PROFIT.

It had belonged to her great aunt Celia, who flew
away on a vacuum cleaner one day - not having any
broomsticks on hand - and was never seen again.
Mrs. Beggs put on the costume, which was a
little too large, and sat down to read the
instruction booklet.

"There," she said. "I hope this will do
the trick." Then she chanted, ever so quietly,

"I've had blizzards,
 Snakes and lizards.
 I've had rain and wind to bear."

As she spoke, the room filled with smoke.

"I've heard noise and lots of howling,
 Tables floating through the air."

Bats darted through the room and strange things
peered from the dark.

"Powers creeping, I command you.
 Get this wizard out of here!"

With a howl the roomful of strange things dashed
through the window and were gone.
Putting everything neatly away, Mrs. Beggs went
to bed.

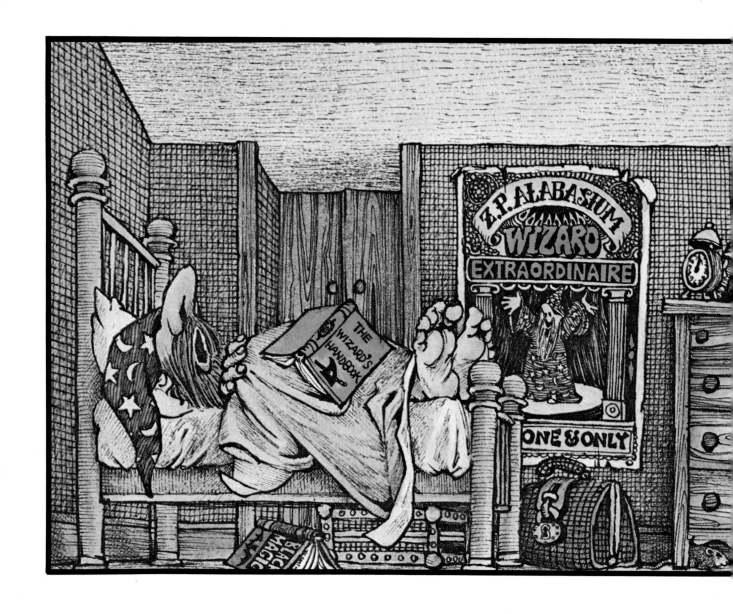

Later that evening Mr. Alabasium slept well.
The window to his room slid slowly open.

Quietly, ever so quietly, in crept a group
of very strange things.

They tied him up with a wizard-proof rope.
They tickled his toes and tweaked his nose.

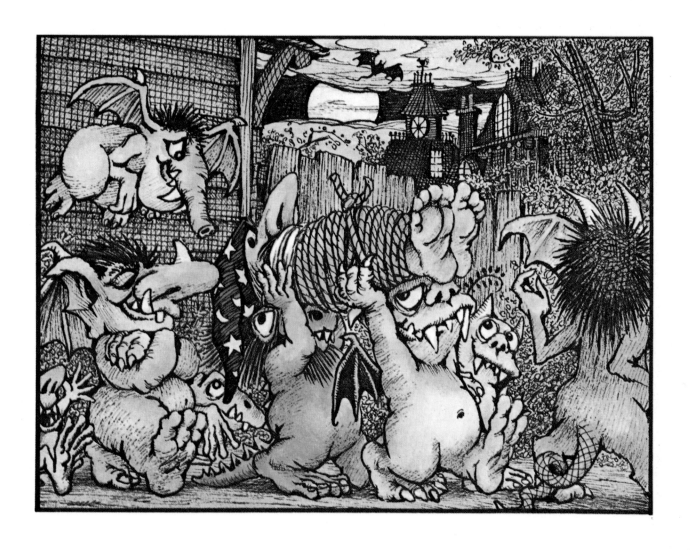

They carried him quietly out of the house and
through the back streets of the town.

They left Z.P. ALABASIUM, *Wizard Extraordinaire,*
at the city dump and flew off in the night.

The next day, when nothing strange happened
at the boarding house, the guests were overjoyed.
"My, my, it's so very peaceful around here,"
commented Mrs. Fizzle.
"It most certainly is," replied the other guests,
smiling their approval.
By late afternoon, Major Clearlob sighed and said,
"It's far too peaceful around here. I'm bored to tears."
"So are we," the others replied.
At dinnertime, everyone quietly sipped their soup.
Then the doorbell rang.
"I wonder who that could be at this hour,"
said Mrs. Beggs, and she went to answer the door.

THE END